Garbage Trucks

Quinn M. Arnold

seedlings

CREATIVE EDUCATION • CREATIVE PAPERBACKS

Published by Creative Education and Creative Paperbacks
P.O. Box 227, Mankato, Minnesota 56002
Creative Education and Creative Paperbacks
are imprints of The Creative Company
www.thecreativecompany.us

Design by Ellen Huber; production by Joe Kahnke
Art direction by Rita Marshall
Printed in the United States of America

Photographs by 123rf (Robert Wilson), Alamy (Agencja
Fotograficzna Caro, A. T. Willett), Corbis (Don Mason/Spaces
Images, Steven Vidler), Dreamstime (Paul Hakimata, Konstantinos
Moraitis, Robwilson39, Dmitriy Sladkov, Typhoonski, Uatp1),
iStockphoto (kozmoat98, PeopleImages, vm), Shutterstock (Johnny
Habell, Cary Kalscheuer, KPG_Payless, Taina Sohlman, Aleksey
Stemmer)

Library of Congress Cataloging-in-Publication Data
Arnold, Quinn M.
Garbage trucks / Quinn M. Arnold.
p. cm. — (Seedlings)
Includes bibliographical references and index.
Summary: A kindergarten-level introduction to garbage
trucks, covering their purpose, where they are found, the
people who work with them, and such defining features as
their hoppers.
ISBN 978-1-60818-790-4 (hardcover)
ISBN 978-1-62832-386-3 (pbk)
ISBN 978-1-56660-820-6 (eBook)
This title has been submitted for
CIP processing under LCCN 2016937137.

CCSS: RI.K.1, 2, 3, 4, 5, 6, 7;
RI.1.1, 2, 3, 4, 5, 6, 7; RF.K.1, 3; RF.1.1

First Edition HC 9 8 7 6 5 4 3 2 1
First Edition PBK 9 8 7 6 5 4 3 2 1

TABLE OF CONTENTS

Hello, garbage trucks!

Garbage trucks
are big trucks.
They drive on
city streets and
country roads.

The front of a garbage truck is the cab. The driver sits there.

A helper rides along. This person loads trash.

The hopper is the back of the truck. It holds garbage. A packer blade crushes the trash inside.

Now there is
room for more.

Most garbage
trucks load at the
tailgate. Others
load from the front.

Some use a side arm.

A garbage truck can have 10 wheels! It holds more than 12 tons of trash.

Garbage trucks pick up trash.

They take it to landfills.

Goodbye, garbage trucks!

Picture a Garbage Truck

hopper

exhaust pipe

cab

packer blade

trash

tailgate

wheel

landfills: large areas where trash is covered with dirt

tailgate: the end of a garbage truck that can be raised

Read More

Lindeen, Mary. *Garbage Trucks*.
Minneapolis: Bellwether Media, 2008.

Meister, Cari. *Garbage Trucks*.
Minneapolis: Jump!, 2014.

Websites

Enchanted Learning
http://www.enchantedlearning.com/paint/vehicles
/garbagetruck.shtml
"Paint" a garbage truck using this online tool.

Garbage Truck Number Recognition
http://schoolhousetoys.com/garbage-truck
-number-recognition/
Use numbered garbage trucks to practice counting.

Index